Carmel Harrington is a bestselling and award-winning author from Ireland. Her novel *The Stolen Child* was an *Irish Times* No. 1 bestseller, was shortlisted for the Irish Book Awards Crime Fiction Book of the Year, and was a *Good Housekeeping* Good Books winner. Carmel is a regular on Irish television and radio, and has been a guest speaker at literary events in Ireland, the UK and the USA. She lives in Wexford with her husband, children and rescue dog George Bailey.

By Carmel Harrington

The Last Bench

The Nowhere Girls

The Stolen Child

The Lighthouse Secret

The Girl from Donegal

A Mother's Heart

The Moon Over Kilmore Quay

My Pear-Shaped Life

A Thousand Roads Home

Cold Feet: The Lost Years

The Woman at 72 Derry Lane

The Things I Should Have Told You

Every Time a Bell Rings

The Life You Left

Beyond Grace's Rainbow

Carmel Harrington
the Last Bench

REVIEW

Family, like branches on a tree, we grow in different directions, yet our roots remain as one.

For the Original O'Gradys
Tina, Michael, Fiona, John, Michelle (and me!)

*'With every morn their love grew tenderer,
with every eve deeper and tenderer still'*

– 'Isabella, or the Pot of Basil'
John Keats

One
Vega

7 April 2025

Vega began walking along the trail at Carrigfoyle, a local beauty spot. She nodded as she passed several dog walkers and a young couple who were holding hands, beaming at the world and each other. She smiled back, thinking of her boyfriend, Luka. He'd like it here. Her favourite bench was free, so she sat down and took a sip of her takeaway coffee. The stunning vista of the Wexford countryside beneath her, centred around a beautiful lake, still took her breath away.

Vega pulled her mobile from her pocket and dialled Kieran's number. Her editor at *Ireland Today*, the newspaper where she worked as an investigative journalist, answered immediately.

'Hey, kiddo.' His voice sounded scratchy, and he cleared his throat before adding, 'You okay?'

'Never mind me. How are you? Vega asked, her forehead creased in concern.

Kieran was at home, on sick leave, recovering from a bout of flu that had knocked him sideways and raised his blood pressure to dangerous levels. During her time at the newspaper, he'd never missed a day.

'I'm grand. Can't keep an old dog like me down. Sorry I'm missing today.'

Vega and Kieran had a long-standing tradition of meeting in his office every Monday morning with coffee. He'd go through her submitted copy, and they'd discuss ideas for new stories.

'Never mind that. Just get better soon. Besides, I've got the best view in town here.' She took a photo and pinged it across to him.

'And here I was feeling bad about missing our meeting,' Kieran said with a chuckle. 'Fill me in on where you are on that drugs story.'

Vega gathered her thoughts about the investigative piece she was writing on the widespread use of drugs in rural communities. 'It's evolved from my initial pitch to you. I know the plan was to focus on the current drugs crisis, but, from the interviews I've completed, the story keeps bringing me back to the nineties.'

'Who have you spoken to?'

'A recovered addict, a dealer – who, of course, wants to remain anonymous – and a couple whose son died from an overdose in 1997.'

'What age was he?' Kieran asked.

'His name was Stephen Grant and he was only eighteen. The dealer who supplied him with the drugs was arrested, though, and there was a court case in 1998. Looking into that has sent me down a whole new rabbit hole.' She flicked through her notes. 'The dealer prosecuted went by the name Hinges. He got the nickname because he spent years as a bouncer working every nightclub and pub door in Wexford. Until it was discovered that, besides throwing people out, he was also selling drugs. His name came up so many times in my research that it caught my interest. But I've been unable to locate him.'

'I take it he was acquitted?'

'Yes and no. He got off on a technicality.'

'Maybe he doesn't want to be found.'

'I know, but . . .' Vega sighed. 'I feel there's a story here.'

'Then you need to trust your instincts and keep looking.'

'I'm glad you said that! I found an on/off girlfriend of his, Julie, who said the last time she saw him was in August 1998. She was still annoyed with him for standing her up for a date. But she did say that Hinges had form, though, for disappearing for months at a time when he ran into trouble.' Vega frowned. 'She reckons he's either started a new life in Spain, something he threatened to do, or he's dead.'

'Any other family members?'

'His parents are dead. No siblings. But . . . I'm about to interview another family who lost a child to an overdose back in 1992. The Grants suggested I talk to them.'

'I see what you mean about the story pushing you back decades.' Kieran paused, then asked, 'So you think this couple know Hinges?'

'Well, they never missed a day in court during Hinges's trial, so they were invested. I'd like to hear what they have to say. It might be another dead end, but they've raised tens of thousands for Aiséirí, a local addiction treatment centre for adults and teens. Tragedy leading to good might be a nice feel-good addition for the article too.'

'I agree. How did they raise the money?'

'They created a small maze of blossom trees at the top of their garden. They open it up to the public for donations every weekend in the spring.'

'Good for them. Why don't you give me a call this afternoon to let me know if they can point you in Hinges's direction. If anyone can find him, you will. You've proved that, kiddo,' Kieran said warmly.

Vega could hear the smile in his voice. Last year had been a life-changing one for her. She'd been on a quest to find two missing children, who were dubbed *The Nowhere Girls* in the media. When she found them, she found herself too.

'If he's out there, I'll get him.' Vega said firmly. She drained the last of her coffee and stood up. 'I'd better go. Promise me you'll take it easy. You're pretty important to me.'

'Don't you worry, kiddo. I'm not going anywhere.'

Ten minutes later, Vega pulled her Kia into the driveway of a pristine white 1980s bungalow, nestled among a mature garden of trees and shrubs on Forth Mountain. Vega checked her phone was fully charged, ready to record her interview with Anne and John Davis. As she approached their front door, she felt a familiar and welcome sensation wash over her – a heightened awareness where all her senses sharpened, signalling she was on the verge of a story breakthrough.

It was time to find out what the Davises had to say.

Two

Anne

'I'm still not convinced this interview is the right thing to do,' John said, pacing the marble tiles in their kitchen.

'Nor am I. But we've committed ourselves now,' Anne replied as she placed a lemon drizzle cake in the centre of their kitchen island. She licked icing from her fingertips, nodding in satisfaction as the sweetness hit her tongue.

'Remind me again why I agreed to this,' John muttered in protest, all the while eyeing his wife's signature bake appreciatively.

'We've been through this several times. Vega Pearse is writing an exposé on the growing drug situation in Wexford, over the past thirty years. With or without our input. Elaine Grant said she asked a lot of questions about Hinges. We need to find out exactly what she's writing about.'

'But we agreed years ago never to be interviewed,' John said, his voice low.

Anne approached his side and clasped his hands firmly in her own. 'If trouble is coming to our door, I want to be ready for it.'

'We've always said we wouldn't meet trouble halfway, Anne. This feels very much like that.'

The sound of their doorbell ringing startled them. There was no time to dwell further.

'Think before you speak,' John said, grabbing Anne's arm. She nodded, then wiped her hands on her trousers before walking to open the door.

The journalist's eyes were wide and bright as she shook hands. She was a pretty girl, with a short haircut that would have looked masculine on most women, but somehow radiated femininity on Vega. She wore a battered black biker jacket over jeans, and seemed very cool.

'Hi, I'm Vega Pearse. It's nice to meet you both.'

'Come on in. You're welcome,' Anne said, and they returned to the kitchen.

'It smells gorgeous here!' Vega said, sniffing the air appreciatively.

'There's always cake on the go for visitors,' Anne replied. 'But I thought we'd start with the tour first.'

'I'm happy to follow your lead,' Vega said, her voice warm. 'I want this to be comfortable for you both. As I said on the phone, we'll take this at your pace.'

John frowned and Vega caught it.

'I can see you're still unsure. I was a little surprised when you agreed to meet me, when I heard you'd turned down all interviews in the past.'

John locked eyes with Anne and nodded at her as if to say, 'You wanted this, so this is yours to answer.'

'We're private individuals and have never felt the need to share our story publicly,' Anne said.

'You haven't been on record about your impressive fundraising before,' Vega stated.

Anne shrugged. 'The donations and the money raised have been a great comfort to us, but we don't want any recognition for it.'

John nodded vigorously at his wife, adding, 'We didn't start all of this to get pats on the back. Don't be waxing lyrical about us two in whatever you write. Keep it to the facts on how to donate.'

'Got it,' Vega replied. 'Can I ask why you said yes to me?'

'We've read your articles,' Anne replied. 'I like that you don't judge, just listen and write with empathy.'

Anne appreciated that Vega took the time to make eye contact with them both, before she replied, 'Thank you for trusting me. I promise

I'm not interested in sensationalism. My only interest is reporting the truth of any situation. You're in safe hands.'

John's jaw clenched, and he turned his back on them.

Anne could see how difficult this was for him. Talking about their lives before and after 1992 was going to dredge up emotions that both of them found challenging.

And, goodness knows, he had been a pillar of strength for them all far too often.

Her rock.

Anne was sure of one thing, though. If the truth came tumbling out, then she would step up. It was her turn to be courageous now.

Three

Anne

25 August 1998

Anne heard the car door slam. John was home. She looked down at her hands, which were still trembling.

'Damn it.' She cursed out loud at her body's betrayal. If she had any chance at pulling this off, she couldn't show any weakness to John.

Or to him.

She glanced at the back door, picked up her glass of whiskey, and drained the measure in one sharp gulp. Then she moved to the front door to greet her husband, checking that the electronic gates at the end of the driveway were closing behind him.

John took one look at her and asked, 'What's wrong?'

That was the problem with spending your entire life with one person – they knew you too well, despite your best efforts to mask your emotions.

'I need you to stay calm, but there's been a development.'

John's jaw clenched, and he moved closer to Anne. 'What kind of development?'

'I don't want you to worry.'

He ignored her. 'What have you done, Anne?'

John seldom got cross with her. He was a gentle soul who devoted his life to making hers better. Whereas she was known for her impulsive tendencies. She hated the thought of being the cause of more distress for him. They had experienced more in their lifetime than most.

'You'd better come with me.' Anne led the way towards the kitchen, her husband's footsteps echoing behind her. His worry and fear filled the air. She turned to him and whispered, 'I promise you that I have a plan. Do you trust me?'

He nodded warily.

Anne understood. Until he saw what they were dealing with, she couldn't expect him to behave any differently. She opened the back door and moved aside so he could see for himself.

'What the f—' John exploded, then took a step back, as if unable to comprehend what lay before him.

Half lying, half sitting, bound and gagged in their garden wheelbarrow, was Hinges.

A man who had destroyed their lives without thought or regret.

His eyes were wide, but not filled with any fear. He was angry. Despite his gag, he tried his best to cry out, letting out muffled moans as he struggled against his restraints.

'I've double-knotted everything. He's not getting out,' Anne said reassuringly to her husband. She glanced at John again, trying to judge his mood.

He leaned against the back doorframe. And who could blame him?

'The thing is, I couldn't get him up the back door step. No matter how many times I tried, I didn't have the strength to move the wheelbarrow up and over. You know my back gives me trouble. I thought it best to leave him here until you got home.' Anne reached over and touched John's arm lightly. 'Could you push him up on to the step and into the kitchen for me? I think we should get him inside. In case someone comes to the back door. I know it's unlikely, as the gate is closed now. But even so. Better be careful in these situations.'

'In *these* situations?' John exclaimed, colour rising in his cheeks. 'When have we ever had a situation like this before? What in God's name... I mean, I can't... I don't... Anne, what have you done?' John spluttered in stops and starts.

Anne nodded sympathetically. She genuinely felt bad for springing this on her husband. But it was better this way. He would have talked her out of it if she had shared her plan.

'Bring Hinges inside, and I'll tell you everything.'

Anne watched her husband's face as he grappled with his options. And to John's credit, without any further argument, he picked up the handles of the wheelbarrow, tipping it and a still moaning Hinges back, until the front wheel was on top of the step to the house. Then he pushed it inside.

'You made that look easy,' Anne said admiringly. Today she felt every bit of her forty-seven years, while John never seemed to age, despite being close to fifty. 'Honestly, I'd have been here all night trying to do the same. He's heavier than he looks.' She grabbed the bottle of Jameson whiskey and poured John a glass. 'Sip this. It will help. You've had a shock.'

John waved aside the drink, as Hinges made another attempt to speak. She could pick out a couple of the choice words he was calling her, despite the gag. She turned to him and said wearily, 'Oh, do shut up. I've told you already there's no point fussing. When we're ready to talk to you, I'll take the gag off and you can let loose!' Then she returned her attention to her husband and said, 'I had to take him.'

John pulled her by her arm into the hallway, closing the door to the kitchen behind them. 'Have you lost your mind?'

'I've never felt saner in my entire life,' Anne replied. She looked down at her hands – and, of course, there was no more trembling. Partly because now John was with her, and she knew that with him at her side she might pull this off. But also because she was finally doing something. For too long, they had been living a nightmare that no parent should ever bear.

Stuck. Unmoving. Powerless.

But no more.

Four

John

John dug his fingernails into the palm of his hand. That's what they told you to do when you were caught in a nightmare. To check whether the situation was real or not. Wake you the hell up.

'Is that the man who murdered our child sitting in a wheelbarrow in our kitchen?' John asked, his voice low and far calmer than it had any right to be. A bead of sweat trickled down his back, and he shrugged off his suit jacket, letting it drop to the ground.

Anne picked up the jacket, smoothed it with her hands, then hung it on the handle on the back of the bathroom door. All the while, she watched him, her eyes wide and glistening in her flushed face.

He raised an eyebrow and asked again, 'Anne?'
'Yes, that's the man.'
So there was no waking up from this.

He cursed again, running his hands through his hair. Anne said she had a plan. But before he questioned her about that he needed to understand how the hell his sixty-kilo wife managed to get a six-foot man, at least fifty kilograms heavier, bound and gagged to their home. 'How did you do it?'

'It wasn't on a whim. I've been planning this for several months, ever since Hinges's trial,' Anne admitted. She lifted her chin, and John could see pride in her eyes. 'While you were in the office, I've been monitoring his movements. Following him. Watching him.' She walked into the kitchen, returning with her handbag a moment later, and pulled out a pink notebook with a detailed gold leaf pattern on it. 'See,' she said, showing it to him.

Written in her neat handwriting, Anne had carefully listed Hinges's whereabouts by date and time. He flicked through the pages, dozens of them. On every page, there were a couple of items circled.

'Where I could identify a pattern, I marked it,' Anne explained.

'Christ Almighty,' John said, shaking his head in disbelief. He'd seen her with the notebook over the past few weeks and had assumed she'd started writing her Christmas shopping list. She sometimes did that – buying presents for their kids, ready for when they came home from university. 'This is insane, Anne.'

She shrugged. 'I've never felt saner. I was careful, John. I took no chances and knew the best chance of catching him was on a Thursday.'

John felt a stabbing pain under his ribcage. Was he having a heart attack? 'I cannot believe what I'm hearing.'

Anne lightly touched his arm. 'I was cautious. He never saw me. Last week, I thought he might have copped me. I was hiding behind a group of teenagers on the main street. He was heading up the Opera House laneway. Anyhow, he turned round, looking all around him. When he locked eyes with me, he threw his gaze upwards and dismissed me in a flash. To him, I was a middle-aged lady. Forgettable. Not a threat.'

John thought he knew his wife better than anyone else on this planet, but clearly not. 'Okay, get to how you got him from wherever he was to here,' John said, his voice clipped, edged with tension.

'I'm coming to that. As I said, once I realised that Hinges follows a similar pattern each week, I came up with a plan. On Thursdays, he has a regular meet-up with several customers in a car park – you know the big one behind that supermarket that closed down last year, the one on that road near the church in Wexford. We parked there once when we couldn't get a spot for that show in the Opera House.'

John nodded. Typical Anne, who never knew the names of buildings or roads. He'd always thought of her fondly as a little scatty. His eyes darted to the door of the kitchen, and he opened it quickly to check on Hinges.

He was still there. This wasn't a nightmare.

Once John nodded for her to carry on, Anne said, 'Well, he leaves Wexford at three o'clock, picks up an Abrakebabra takeaway, then drives home. He lives down a quiet lane off the N25. It only allows one-way traffic. Tiny.'

John knew where Hinges lived. He'd been there himself six years earlier. Plotting, planning, hating. Until he'd come to his senses and returned home to his grieving family.

'I created a diversion by parking up outside the entrance to the only other house on the lane. The only option for him to get past me was to ask me to move. I had the hazard lights on and sat tight.'

John clutched his chest as another pain struck him. He couldn't believe what he was hearing.

While he was in the office each day, meeting clients, his wife was plotting to do God knows what to a drug dealer.

'He wasn't happy with me. Not a patient man. Anyhow, I told him I was waiting to see the young couple who live down the road from him, who were both at work. And, as I told you, I was careful. I knew that they wouldn't be home from work until at least six thirty.' Anne looked smug with this detail and looked at John expectantly. She wanted him to acknowledge and praise her planning. His head swam, and he wished he'd taken that drink now.

'Anyhow, Hinges told me to get out of his effing way – honestly, the mouth on him, shouting out of his window, honking his horn. I got out and told him my car had a dodgy battery and needed a jump-start, but I didn't know how.' She smiled, 'I told him that the lever to pop the bonnet was on the passenger side. Sure, he had no choice but to help. I knew he wanted to get to his Abrakebabra.' Anne frowned. 'I did consider giving him a belt across the head with the jump-start box. It's heavy enough, and I reckon I could have knocked him out cold with it. But I was worried I might kill him. And I didn't want to kill him.'

'No. That would be ridiculous,' John said sarcastically.

'Exactly. We need him alive. As he sat in the passenger seat, I put a chloroform-drenched rag on his mouth. Got it from a pharmacy. He was out like a light in seconds.'

John felt his jaw slacken as it hit the floor. He'd known Anne for more than forty years, ever since they were children. And there were many times that he'd been surprised by her. But this was new territory.

'Once I'd tied his legs and arms, and knew he couldn't move, even if he woke up before we got home, I moved my car into the entrance of the Fox's bungalow, which gave me the space to drive Hinges's car down the lane to his house. I turned the engine off and threw his keys through the letterbox. Oh, and I took his takeaway, because I was afraid it might look odd if someone saw it uneaten in the car.'

'You thought of everything.'

'I did. I even wore gloves, so that I didn't leave any fingerprints.' Again, that flash of pride on her face, and for a moment, despite himself, John couldn't help but feel impressed with her too.

'I drove home and, honestly, those twenty minutes felt like the longest of my life. I mean, what if we met a Gardaí checkpoint? He looked like he was napping in the passenger seat, but what if he woke up? Thankfully, it was a dream of a drive. As if someone was looking out for me – our guardian angel. I managed to pull him out of the car and into the wheelbarrow. He was still out cold. The back doorstep was tricky for me, as you know. I made myself a cup of tea and watched him from the kitchen window, waiting for him to wake, which was about ten minutes before you got home. I think that's you all caught up!'

John shook his head slowly as he tried to make sense of his wife's words.

'I know it's a shock for you. And you must have lots of questions for me,' Anne said, gently.

There were dozens of questions John could have asked, but only one came to mind, to which he was frankly terrified to hear the answer. Nevertheless, it had to be asked. 'Now that you've got him here, what do you plan to do with him?'

Five

John

7 April 2025

John led the way through their private garden towards the top field. He heard Vega take a sharp breath as she took in the majesty of the landscaping for the first time.

'You did all of this yourself,' Vega said, her eyes flitting around her.

'Every single slab of concrete was cut and laid by John,' Anne said, smiling at her husband. 'There's not much in our house or garden that he didn't have a hand in creating.'

John felt a flush of embarrassment at the praise, coupled with pride. He knew he had accomplished something special here. But he'd had help, especially over the past ten years.

Vega whistled appreciatively, 'I'm not handy at all. I bought a pack of those stick-on picture hangers. No nails. What could go wrong? Well, apparently, a lot.'

They all chuckled at her joke.

'Well, I might be good with a hammer and nail, or a shovel, but Anne is the one with the good eye,' John said. His mind wandered back to his wife, a newly-wed, sewing curtains for their first home – a static caravan – trying to make it look pretty.

'This is a big site. What is it, an acre?' Vega asked.

'Almost one and a half. The house sits on three-quarters of an acre. The rest is in what we have always called the top field, but the public knows as the blossom maze,' Anne said, a little breathlessly.

John frowned, changing his pace for Anne. She had slowed down over the past year, and it worried him. Stairs and hills, once easily tackled, now made her hesitate. He had insisted she visit their doctor for a complete check-up. Everything was fine apart from her blood pressure, which occasionally acted up – nothing to worry about, bar the usual complaints of someone slowing down in their seventies.

'You can see the sea!' Vega exclaimed, stopping and turning round to take in the coastline.

'Yes, and you can see the Saltee Islands from our bedroom,' Anne said. She waved her hand towards their right. 'That's Rosslare Harbour over there. And to your left is Forth Mountain.'

'Honestly, I've always believed my cottage in the Ballagh to be one of the prettiest places on earth. But this is special. I bet you get asked to sell often. Properties like this are so rare!'

'We'll never sell,' John stated bluntly, looking away quickly when he saw Vega's look of surprise.

'A lifetime of family memories here,' Anne added. 'We could never give this up. And we hope that, one day, one of our children will make it their family home.'

They reached the top of their garden, and John led the way behind a row of whitewashed sheds. 'These used to be stables. The kids had ponies growing up. Now, it's home to the ride-on lawnmower,' John said.

'No need for a riding hat for that,' Anne joked.

'This entrance to the top field is for us only. When we open the garden to the public at weekends, they enter through a separate gate, accessible down a lane adjacent to our house,' John explained.

They turned round the gable end of the stable,

and he waited for a gasp of wonder from Vega. She didn't disappoint.

'I've never seen anything like this,' Vega exclaimed, walking closer, her eyes moving from left to right.

The large, lush, green field was situated on a gentle slope, with the backdrop of Forth Mountain behind it. To the right was a small gravelled area for parking. The wrought-iron gate at the public entrance was closed, but would open on Saturday for the first time this season, remaining open until the last buds fell from the trees.

But what demanded all their attention was the maze at the centre of the field, created with tall blossom trees in full bloom, forming a canopy of pink and white flowers that cascaded over a winding gravel pathway. They ranged from one to ten metres tall and solar lanterns were embedded in the ground every few metres, a relatively recent addition but one that significantly improved the garden. Now, John and Anne could enjoy the space late into the evenings.

'I feel like I'm in a dream,' Vega said, her voice cracking. 'I've seen photographs, but, honestly, none of them do this justice.'

John nodded in satisfaction, her reaction pleasing him.

'How many trees are there?' Vega asked.

'Over two hundred blossom trees, in –' he paused to think – 'in six different varieties. I'll show you all of them as we wander around. Let's see if you can find the first bench without going wrong.' John offered his arm to Anne, and at first he thought she'd refuse it, as she was stubborn and independent, often averse to help. But her face softened, and she whispered a thank you as she clasped his arm.

'How long has the maze taken you to build?' Vega asked, taking the lead in front of them.

'Twenty-six years, seven months and twelve days,' Anne said, her hand tightening its grip on his arm.

John felt an ache in his chest, that his wife was aware of this fact, that even on the days she didn't talk about 1998 it didn't mean she wasn't thinking about it.

'That's very precise,' Vega said, turning round to look at them, eyebrows raised in surprise.

'I'm good with dates,' Anne mumbled back. 'Keep going, dear.' She ushered Vega forward until the path reached a fork.

'So, do we go right or left?' Vega asked, her eyes shining bright.

'Your choice,' John said. That was the thing with mazes, he thought. They always brought out a person's inner child. And for a moment he heard the echoes of his children's delight as they ran through the Japanese Garden at Powerscourt. If only they could go back to that time. He sighed, wishing he had realised how special those little moments were at the time so that he could have enjoyed them more.

Anne looked at him knowingly, and he leaned down to kiss the top of her greying brown hair.

Vega peered down each pathway, then lifted her eyes towards the sky. 'I like how the sunlight filters through the leaves on the left side. This way!'

'I like that too,' Anne agreed. 'I always look out for new patterns when I come up here, cast by the sun and shadow. They change every time.'

They followed Vega, and she let out a slight squeal when she reached a circular metal tree bench, which sat beneath a tall cherry blossom.

'Well done! You've come to the first bench. And the *Prunus* "Kanzan", which is probably the most famous of the Japanese flowering cherries,' John said. 'It always gives these deep pink double flowers, with bronze leaves. I've about a dozen of these scattered throughout the garden.'

'And the leaves turn a brilliant orange in the autumn,' Anne added.

'How do you remember which tree is which?' Vega asked incredulously.

'They all have their own special features. The Kanzan's bark has a coppery sheen, and the leaves are oval-shaped,' Anne said. She took a seat on the bench.

'You take the other seat,' John said to Vega, quickly waving aside her protests.

'This looks antique,' Vega said, running her hand over the cream paintwork of the bench.

'It is!' John replied. 'It was my grandparents before it became ours, and it was also the first place I ever kissed Anne.'

Six

Vega

Vega had been observing the couple closely over the past thirty minutes. It was clear they shared a deep affection. From John's kind gesture of offering his arm to help Anne on the uneven path, to the way Anne looked at him with evident pride as he guided them through his creation.

However, even though she liked them a great deal, she noticed a few things that made her pause.

That they knew the exact day they began making this maze was interesting. She couldn't give a precise timeline for when she bought her cottage, which was the biggest thing she'd ever owned. She thought of Luka. Yes, Vega could say they had been together for eighteen months. But she couldn't specify the exact length, whether months, weeks or days, as the Davises could with this maze. Curious. Also, the way

John responded to her suggestion of selling. His reply had been firm and swift. Yes, understandable that he wouldn't want to sell a family home. But the way he'd answered her so gruffly was puzzling.

Vega's mind raced through half a dozen questions she for which she was eager to get answers. But she recalled Anne's terms for their interview, insisting that she must let them tell their story, their way, so, instead, she prompted them to continue: 'What age were you both for this first kiss?'

Anne's eyes sparkled as she spoke. 'I was six years old, and John would have been eight!' Anne said, giggling. 'When we say that we were childhood sweethearts, we mean it!'

'My grandfather bought this bench for my grandmother. She was a keen reader and always engrossed in a good mystery, sitting on this, with a rug over her knees. That's how I remember her,' John said. 'Clever woman too – she had a great mind and wit. Anyhow, this was under a willow tree in front of their farmhouse. The branches hung so low that we loved playing underneath them. It felt like a little hidden den.'

Anne interrupted to continue with the story. 'I'd been to the farm for the first time for a playdate with John's sister. I had never been on a farm before. It was like stepping on to a movie set. Anyway, we were playing a game of hide-and-seek, all of us kids together . . .'

'My cousins,' John explained. 'My aunts and uncle also built their homes on my grandparents' land, which meant there was always someone to play with on the farm. We had a lot of fun back then; every day felt like a new adventure.'

'Until I nearly died!' Anne exclaimed, cutting in dramatically.

'Whoa! This is taking a turn,' Vega said, enjoying their tale, which they'd clearly shared many times over the years.

'I was searching for a place to hide. I took what I believed was a shortcut to a field. I climbed over a gate and started to run across the concrete . . .' Anne said.

'. . . but it wasn't concrete. It was a slurry tank,' John cut in. 'The top had hardened in the sun. I suppose to a city kid . . . Well, how would they know?'

'I screamed as I started to sink, thinking I was in quicksand! The smell . . .' Anne wrinkled her nose at the memory.

'I nearly had a heart attack when I saw her head, barely visible above the slurry. I jumped on the gate, used my legs to swing it over the slurry pit, grabbed Anne by the scruff of her neck and yanked her up!'

'My hero!' Anne said, looking up to him. 'Then and now.'

Vega's heart swelled as she listened to Anne and John talk. Their love was adorable to witness. She couldn't wait to tell Luka about them later. He was such an old romantic.

'You were lucky you survived that!' Vega said, her mind turning to recent news where toxic gases from a slurry tank had killed farmers.

'I was grand,' Anne said, shrugging. 'John hosed me down, and I smelled pretty bad for a few days, no matter how many baths I took. But not a bother on me.'

'She's tough. Always has been,' John agreed with the same pride.

'Well, as he saved my life, I kissed him and told him I'd marry him some day. And you know what, that kiss sealed our future. It was the first step in what we've always believed was fate.' Anne paused, colouring slightly. 'You probably don't believe in fate . . .'

Vega raised her hand and swiftly interrupted. 'I spent most of my life being a cynic, but last year fate literally put me in front of someone I'd been searching for throughout my entire adult life. I refuse to believe that something higher than me didn't play a part in reconnecting us. You could call that fate too, but I've always thought of it as the stars aligning.'

John smiled at Vega, which felt like a breakthrough. 'That's a nice thought. Well, I'll be forever grateful that stars put Anne in my path.'

'I can't wait to hear the rest of your story,' Vega said truthfully. 'How long have you been together?'

'That first kiss was almost seventy years ago. But it took us a decade to make it official, which means we've been a couple for sixty years now.' Anne said.

'My mind is officially blown at that thought. To find someone you love at such an early age, and spend a lifetime together... It's couple goals! What's your secret?' Vega asked.

'Love. Simple as that,' Anne said, without hesitation. 'We've had a good life, but parts of it have been incredibly heartbreaking. The kind of sorrow that rips right through a family, tearing them apart. Love was the glue that held us together. Through thick and thin. I know there were times when John didn't like how I behaved, disagreed with my impulsivity, but he never stopped loving me.'

Anne and John shared another of their knowing glances. Vega sensed they were concealing a great deal. What secrets did these two hold?

'There's nothing you could do to make me stop loving you,' John said, picking up Anne's hand and kissing it lightly. He turned to Vega and added, 'Anne has summed it all up beautifully. But I'll add this, which is what I shared in my wedding speech for each of my kids when they got married: there will be days when it's easy to love each other – treasure them. But in the dark moments you need to show up for each other. Because it will seem easier to walk away. Fight for your marriage. And never quit loving one another.'

Vega slumped back into the bench, exhaling deeply. 'That's powerful. Thank you. I'll carry that advice with me always.'

But her mind went back to two words John had said.

Dark moments.

The more this lovely couple spoke, the more her gut instinct told her that there was a story, hidden, lurking in the background.

Seven

Anne

25 August 1998

Anne insisted that John have that shot of whiskey. He had gone as white as a sheet as she recounted her steps to kidnap Hinges. They were still huddled in the corner of their hallway, but at least while he sipped his drink the colour returned to his cheeks.

'What's your big plan, then, Anne?'

'I want him to confess. To us, the Grants and the hundreds of kids he's helped on their way to addiction.'

John nodded, understanding this need. 'Then what?'

'Well, I've got our camcorder hidden behind my cookbooks on the dresser. I'll switch it on when we go in.'

'And you think that he's going to admit what he's done?' John asked incredulously.

'Probably not. We'll need to offer him some incentive. I thought you could do that.'

'I assume you've figured out how I'll do that too?'

Anne didn't appreciate the sarcastic tone her husband had taken. But she decided to give him a pass. He was still adjusting to their situation here. She flashed John her brightest smile. 'I've made a list.' She opened her pink notebook again. 'We'll do good cop, bad cop. He hates me already, so I might as well stick with the bad-cop role. You can pretend to be on his side.' She flicked through the pages towards the middle of the notebook and found the page she was searching for. She began to read the tips she'd listed down. 'Stay calm. Speak to him in a gentle tone of voice. Make him trust you. You can give him some water. Just a sip now, because we might need to use thirst and hunger as a method of persuasion. He didn't get to eat his Abrakebabra earlier. I bet that's annoying him.'

John rolled his eyes as she snapped her notebook shut.

'And if my gentle tone doesn't make him open up, what then?'

'Time for the bad cop, of course!' Anne said. Honestly, she would have thought that was obvious. 'If you can't get him to talk, then I'll tell him that I'm going to kill him.' Anne felt a shiver run down her spine, and her damn hands began to shake again. She shoved them behind her back quickly.

John's face crumpled, and for a moment she thought her big bear of a husband might weep.

'This isn't you, Anne,' John said softly.

'Oh, but it is, John,' she sighed. She thought about the years she had spent dreaming of seeing that man meet his end. 'It won't be difficult to persuade Hinges that I am serious. Some days, the idea of killing him is the only thing that keeps me going. And don't tell me you haven't thought the same.'

The flicker in John's eyes confirmed her words. He moved towards Anne and gently lifted her chin with his hand. 'Doesn't matter what we have both thought, we are not going to kill him. That's not who we are.'

Anne sighed, hearing the truth in John's words. 'No, we're not killers. But the point is that he doesn't need to know that. He simply has to believe we would.'

John pinched the bridge of his nose as he paced the narrow hallway. 'Even if he confesses, and we give the evidence to the Gardaí, and they charge him, his lawyers will say it's inadmissible, because it was made under duress. Not to mention the fact that we'll face charges for kidnapping. Damn it, Anne, you haven't thought this through.'

That was unfair, because all Anne had done was think about this. Days, weeks, months, years of doing nothing but contemplating how to make that man pay for what he had done.

'When we buried our child, our hearts were shattered into countless pieces. He broke me. Us. Our family. I need to find a way to bring us back together. For the kids,' Anne said. 'We've already lost one, and if we don't make a change we'll lose the other three.' She brushed away a tear tracing down her cheek, then bit her lip until it bruised, the pain stopping her emotion from getting away from her.

'And do you think his owning up to his sins will help you move on?' John asked, his voice heavy with concern.

Truthfully, Anne had no idea. But she had to find a way forward, and this felt like her only option. She moved closer to John and admitted in a whisper, 'I'm scared.'

'Of him?' John asked, nodding towards the kitchen.

She shook her head. 'No. *Of me.* Who I've become.' Anne took a deep breath, gathering her thoughts so she could find the words. 'Michael left because he couldn't cope with us any more. And when the girls come home from college, sharing their lives with us, I sit and nod, smile at the right moments, ask all the right questions. But I'm not truly present. I'm a shell of myself – they deserve better than that.'

Her husband considered her words and Anne saw understanding in his eyes. Because it wasn't just Anne who was moving through life as a shadow of their former self.

'Don't you see, John? We need to confront Hinges. Make him realise what he's cost us. And maybe we can get through to him, find a way to make him stop.'

John pulled her into his arms and held her tightly in an embrace that their bodies instinctively recognised. Anne closed her eyes and searched for a cherished memory on which to anchor herself.

She remembered how they'd held a barbecue every year. In 1992, it had been so hot that everyone was in shorts and T-shirts. Mary, Margaret and Frances were lying down, trying to catch the rays and get a suntan. But Michael had other ideas and turned the hose on them. Chaos ensued as a water fight began, leaving all six of them crying with laughter.

It had been the most perfect of days.

The last day that they were all together before six became five.

Before . . .

John released her, and she returned to their reality, feeling stronger again. She needed John; she couldn't do this on her own. But if she had to she would.

'I thought the only thing I had to worry about this evening was mowing the grass,' John said, pulling a face. He looked calmer too, at the very least, resigned to their situation. He was coming round. She could tell.

'Look, I've got a lamb casserole in the slow cooker and the meat will melt in your mouth. I say we get this over and done with. Get Hinges to confess, let him go and then we'll work out how to tell the Gardaí without leaving ourselves open to too much trouble. With any luck, we can be tucking into our food with a glass of red by the time the news comes on. Sound good?'

John's eyes darkened as he looked at her. 'No, Anne. None of this sounds good. But what choice do I have? You've brought this to our door, and I've got no option but to go along with it.' He tapped the door to the kitchen gently. 'You seem to have forgotten one important factor. That man in there is dangerous. We've seen the destruction he can cause.'

Anne felt sweat begin to pool under her armpits.

John continued, his eyes fixed on the closed door, as if he could see right through the wooden panelling to the other side. 'If I cut his ties to let him go, he will attack us. And while I'm confident I can overpower him, what if he lands a blow to you first? I can't take that risk.'

Her husband was, as always, thinking of her. Anne felt a rush of love overwhelm her for the man she'd shared her heart with, nearly her entire life.

'And what if this confession we hope to get doesn't lead to him going to jail? He'll retaliate. If not immediately, one day I'll come home from work and find you hurt or worse . . .' His voice faltered, and he drained the last of his whiskey.

'He'll talk,' Anne stated, her voice sounding more confident than she felt.

John moaned softly, a gentle sigh of pain echoing down their hallway. 'I wish you'd told me about this. We could have talked it through, come up with something more foolproof.'

'I'm sorry,' Anne said, hanging her head low. 'You don't think there's any chance this can turn out okay?'

He shrugged. 'There's only one way to go now, and that's forward. Come on. Let's get this confession.'

Eight

John

Hinges was fully alert when they returned to the kitchen, his eyes wide as he watched John and Anne. John grasped the handles of the wheelbarrow and moved it to the centre of the kitchen so that it faced the dresser where Anne stood with her back to them, switching on the camcorder as planned, then moving to the left of the dresser.

It was hard to believe that less than two hours ago, John had been wrestling with a box full of receipts from one of his clients' accounts. He locked eyes with Hinges, whose muffled cries continued.

'I'm going to take the gag off,' John said.

Hinges groaned audibly in relief. John held his hand up. 'We live miles from our nearest neighbour. I'm sharing this with you to save you the wasted bother of shouting at the top of your lungs.'

Anne moved closer and said tersely, 'No one can hear your screams here. You'd do well to remember that.'

John glanced at his wife, who was sneering at Hinges with a look of such loathing it should have frightened him. But the thing was he understood that look. He felt the same way, and seeing the man who'd caused them all their heartache sparked anger through his body. But he had to find a way to park that fury. He needed his wits, sharp and calm, to get through this.

John moved forward, and Hinges began to writhe and shake so much inside the barrow that it looked as if it might topple.

'Easy,' John commanded, and to his surprise the man stilled and allowed John to ungag him.

'You've made the biggest mistake of your lives,' Hinges said raspily. 'You better untie me now, before I fucking kill you both.'

John had expected as much from Hinges. 'No shouting or threats, or I'll gag you again.' He held up the rag again, which was damp with Hinge's saliva.

'What do you want?' Hinges replied.

'What do you think we want?' Anne said, her voice tight as she moved closer.

'Drugs, I assume.' His eyes flicked between them both. 'But you don't look the type. Mind you, I see all sorts. Don't judge – that's my motto.' He grinned at them both, as if he expected them to laugh at his intended joke. Shrugging when they didn't smile back, he continued, 'What do you want? If it's cannabis, I'm not your man, but I can sort it for you.'

'We don't want cannabis.' John replied, keeping his voice calm, as Anne's list had advised.

'Oh, something stronger, is it?' Hinges replied. 'Listen, man, let me out of this barrow and I'll hook you up. On the house.'

'What can you hook us up with?' John asked.

'E. Ketamine. Coke. You name it.'

John felt his temples throb as his mind raced through questions he needed to ask, to guide Hinges to where they were supposed to go. 'Where do you sell your drugs?'

Hinges's eyes narrowed. 'What is this? A shakedown from the shades?'

John had not heard that old nickname, used for the Irish Gardaí, for many years. Before he had a chance to refute the allegation, Hinges shook his head, answering his question. 'No way you are the guards.' He looked around the kitchen and smirked. 'From what I can see, you are nothing more than housewife of the year and a pen pusher. Am I right?' He laughed out loud when he clearly saw a flicker of confirmation on their faces. 'When you're right, you're right! So that begs a question: what do you *really* want?'

'Just answer our questions,' Anne shouted at him. 'Starting with, where do you sell your drugs?'

Hinges coughed and then said, 'Throat feels like it's been cut. I need a drink.'

'Nothing until you answer our questions,' Anne said, matching his smirk with one of her own.

John walked to the kitchen cupboard above the sink and pulled out a glass, then reconsidered, thinking it could be used as a weapon of some sort. He opened one of the lower cupboards, nicknamed the party drawer by them all, because it held decorations and paper plates for family celebrations. He found a stack of pink paper cups, pulled one out, filled it with water, held it up and said, 'Answer and it's yours.'

'I meet my regulars in different spots, at different times.' He scoffed, then asked sarcastically, 'You *are* looking for a slot, after all?'

John ignored him and continued to probe, 'What about the pubs and clubs scene? Which of them are you selling in?'

Hinges frowned. 'What's it to you?'

'*Answer!*' Anne yelled.

'Jesus, chill, lady. I don't go near pubs, but

there are a couple of clubs I hit.' He grinned, then added in a decent mimic of Scooby Doo, 'nothing beats a Scooby snack for all the little Freds, Daphnes, Velmas and Shaggys!'

John clenched his fist into a ball, wanting to reach back and, with all his might, knock Hinges's head straight off his skinny little neck. He turned his back on Hinges and looked at Anne, seeing recognition and sympathy in her green eyes. He took several deep breaths then he turned his attention back to Hinges. 'You ever think about how young your customers might be?'

'If they are old enough to be out clubbing, that ain't my business.'

'If they have money, you'll sell to them,' John reaffirmed.

'If I don't, someone else will.' Hinges lifted his chin slightly, daring them to contradict him.

'You must be preparing for a big night tomorrow,' Anne said, her voice low and her face shadowed with hatred. 'With the Leaving Cert results out. New prey for you to sink your teeth into.'

That's why she had done this *today*, John realised. He should have worked it out! She was trying to protect other kids as they hadn't been able to protect their own . . .

'Where's my drink?' Hinges called out, his voice aggrieved.

Unclenching his fist, John grabbed the paper cup of water and threw it in Hinges's face.

He walked over to Anne and whispered, 'I guess it's bad cop, bad cop, after all.'

Nine

Anne

7 April 2025

Anne swallowed a lump in her throat. They hadn't even begun to talk about what had happened in 1992, and already she felt as if she was standing on the edge of an abyss.

'Let's move on to the next bench,' Anne said, standing up. John held out the crook of his elbow again, and she clasped it, giving it an extra squeeze.

'My goodness, I've just noticed the birdsong!' Vega exclaimed.

'You should hear it at dawn. It's a symphony,' John said. 'We've got robins and chaffinches.'

They stopped for a moment.

'That's the robins singing now. Their sound is more gentle, silvery and crystal-like. The chaffinches are more showy,' John stated.

They continued walking in silence, with Vega

only choosing one dead end, before they reached the second bench. Unlike the first antique, this one was more rustic, with three tree trunks used as legs, and a piece of planed wood lying across the top.

'Our son Michael made this when he was thirteen. Had a little help from his dad. I can still see his little face, beaming with pride at his accomplishment! It used to sit in our garden, but we brought it up when we created the maze,' Anne said.

'I love the personal story attached to each bench,' Vega said, taking a seat beside Anne and John. 'When did you get married?'

Anne smiled. 'Well, we got engaged in 1971, once John finished his degree at UCD, and married in 1973. It was a different time. Not like it is for you young people, dating first, then going exclusive, and that's before you even get to boyfriend and girlfriend! You do make it terribly complicated.'

'We skipped all those middle bits and got on with it,' John added with a wink.

'I think you had the right idea,' Vega said, pulling a face. 'I have to admit I was a bit of a slow burner when it came to my boyfriend. It took me a while to put a label on us. I'm lucky he stuck with me.'

'Always worth it when you are with the right person,' John said firmly, looking over to Anne.

He'd clearly forgiven her now for insisting on this interview, Anne thought. He liked Vega too.

'Anne was working as a secretary at a doctor's in Wexford town when I proposed. I took her out for a steak dinner and had the waiter bring out her ring with the dessert. Was quite chuffed with myself for pulling the surprise off!'

'Of course I said yes,' Anne replied.

'And you moved here when you married?' Vega asked.

'Yes. But not this house as you see it. This land was my grandparents'. Their farm was over there.' John pointed to their right. 'They gave us a site, which was a great help. But we didn't have the money to build straight away. We bought a musty old mobile home for £2,300! Had to get a credit union loan to pay for it.' He stood up and waved in front of him. 'I'd say about fifty feet from here, we put it. Anne turned that mobile home into a little palace in no time.'

'Well, John wasn't earning much in the beginning, so I started to do dressmaking. Made graduation dresses and quite a few wedding gowns too. On a Singer sewing machine that used to belong to John's grandmother.' Anne brought her voice down to a whisper, 'Cash in hand.'

Vega whispered back, 'Your secret is safe with me.'

Would all their secrets be safe with Vega, Anne wondered?

'When did you build your house?' Vega asked.

'It took us two years. Brick by brick, all by our own hands, with some help from family. Every night after work, and also on weekends. And in the meantime we had two babies. I brought Mary and Margaret home to that mobile—' Her voice caught, and she looked away.

'When we moved into the house, it was like living in a mansion. So big compared to the mobile. Took us a while to get used to it,' John said.

'Pretty soon after, I was pregnant again, and then again for the fourth time, so the house didn't feel so big any more.'

'It sounds idyllic,' Vega said, with genuine warmth in her voice.

'It was.'

'We missed the simplicity of mobile-home living, so I bought us a caravan. Tiny little thing,' John said.

'We still have our little holiday home. It's in the stables now. We take the grandkids camping in it. It has a set of quad bunk beds that John installed. No headroom, though, and at least one of them would wake up in the morning banging their head.' Anne giggled at the memory. 'But we had fun touring Ireland with that caravan. The six of us, together. Happy days.'

They fell into silence for a moment. Eventually, Anne looked over to John and said, 'If you think about it, it was that caravan that led us to this blossom maze.'

Ten

Vega

Vega was beginning to understand Anne and John. Yes, they were devoted to each other; that was clear. But they'd glance at each other, their eyes would flash with a memory and, without a word, they would decide whether or not to share this part of themselves.

'How did the caravan bring you to this garden?' Vega prompted.

'The kids were all off for Easter break, so we decided to go to Wicklow, staying at a campsite near Powerscourt. We took a day trip to the Japanese Gardens there. Have you been?' Anne asked.

Vega shook her head. As she looked around the beautiful garden she was now in, she instantly added it to her list of places to visit.

'The gardens are pretty, with stone lanterns and pagodas, as well as little Japanese bridges. And, of course, the stunning blossom trees.

Well, they were in full bloom when we got there and, honestly, it was the most wonderful sight to see. We walked down the steps and stood under the trees.' Anne pointed to the grass around them that was dotted with blossoms. 'Like here, the ground was covered in confetti. And Michael, who was a pure devil back then, picked up a handful and threw it at his sisters. Mary and Frances squealed, exactly as he wanted them to. But Margaret beamed with delight as they fell into her hair.'

'I can see her face now; her eyes were always so big on that pale face,' John added.

'She was a fierce romantic. Always reading those teen romances . . . What were they called, John?'

John looked up to the heavens. 'As if I know that . . .'

'You do!' Anne said, then clapped her hands in delight. 'Sweet Valley High. Two sisters, in and out of love, in an American high school. Nonsense, but as sweet as the title. Margaret was addicted to them. Well, standing there in that garden, she announced to us, with the blossoms still in her hair, that one day she would get married, right there in that Japanese garden under the trees.'

'Margaret had this way of telling stories, that

her brother and sisters joined in with her excitement.' John said.

'Mary whipped her sweatshirt off and fashioned it into a veil on Margaret's head. Frances picked a flower and gave it to Margaret for her bouquet. Then the two girls grabbed the bottom of Margaret's skirt and held it up, as if it were a grand, ten-foot train. Michael stood at the top, becoming our priest, then John and I walked Margaret down the aisle. She insisted on both of us!'

John added, 'Michael was only ten, but he bellowed out in a deep voice, "We are gathered here to witness the wedding of Margaret to her imaginary future husband." We all started to laugh. One of those times when you go from funny to hysterical, and before you know it you are clutching each other, with a pain in your stomach from the laughter.'

'I had tears streaming down my face. Then Michael began pegging more blossoms, and we all joined in, until another family came down the stone steps, their eyes wide at the state of us six.'

'Which made us laugh even harder!' John said. 'Oh, you had to be there . . . Must sound silly to you now.'

'No!' Vega replied instantly. 'I wish I had been

there. I mean, what a family to grow up in. Honestly, I should have been so lucky.'

Anne reached over to clasp John's hand. 'That day, that moment in the Japanese garden, captures exactly who we were as a family. Full of teasing, craic, love and laughter. If I could only choose one moment of our life to go back to, it would be that one.'

'Me too,' John said, and he reached up to pull his wife into his arms for a moment, his chin resting on the top of her head.

Their bond and devotion were so intense and magnetic that Vega couldn't tear her eyes away from them.

'That's why you chose a blossom garden,' she said, recognising the significance now.

'Yes. Cherry blossoms were not just Margaret's favourite tree, but also our favourite family memory. Have been ever since that day,' Anne said.

'I couldn't give her that wedding in Powerscourt she dreamed about, but I could give her this at least,' John said, his voice gruff with emotion.

And Vega almost ended the interview at this moment. She wasn't sure she could bear to take them further into their memories. To be the one to make this lovely, kind couple remember why they could never give their daughter the wedding of which she'd dreamed.

To speak of their darkest moment, when their beautiful daughter Margaret had died.

But Vega had to continue probing because she was here not only to find out what had happened to Margaret, but also to see if the Davis family could help her discover where Hinges was.

Eleven

John

'You've only taken one wrong turn,' Anne said approvingly to Vega when she opted to go right at the next crossroads. 'You have good instincts.'

'I think I'd happily get lost in here for a couple of hours,' Vega said. 'I love how you've created these little resting spots throughout the maze, so people can enjoy the blooms. How many benches are there?'

'We've four, but we might add another one this summer. My son and grandson have been plotting,' John said as they reached the next clearing. 'This is the grandkids' favourite.'

He smiled as he watched Vega's face light up, as most people's did, when they came face to face with the treehouse he'd built twelve years ago, when Mary gave them their first grandchild.

'This is brilliant!' Vega exclaimed, looking

upwards. 'That must be over fifteen or twenty metres high!'

'Nearer to thirty now, I'd say,' John replied. 'This tree was already in the field before we decided to start the blossom garden, so it had a head start on the trees we've planted over the past twenty-seven years. Its official name is *Prunus avium* "Plena", but in plain talk it's our native wild cherry. You see them all over Ireland, big spreading trees, and I've planted forty of them in the garden.'

'I love the white double flowers,' Vega said. 'So pretty!'

'You should see them in the autumn – their leaves are a vibrant crimson!' Anne said. 'You'll have to come back. It will be like stepping into a different garden then. The pinks and whites disappear, but reds and oranges take their place. Nature sure is a wonder. And there's no better place to see it all, but from up there.'

All three of them looked upwards. Around the sturdy trunk, about ten metres above the ground, John had built a viewing platform with a wooden ladder for access on one side and a slide on the other for coming down.

'Will we go up?' Anne said with a mischievous glint in her eye.

He was about to give Anne all the reasons

why they should stay on firm ground, let Vega climb on her own, but he could tell by the stubborn tilt of her head that she had her mind made up. 'Okay, but I'll go first, and Vega can follow behind you,' John replied, reaching out a hand to help Anne. She had the occasional dizzy spell due to her blood pressure. He wasn't willing to take any chances that she might fall.

'Oh, you can see everything from here!' Vega said.

'Our grandkids play all sorts up here. Pirates are their favourite at the moment,' Anne said with a grin on her face, thinking of the little ones.

'The bench is a genius addition too! I bet you made all of this yourself,' Vega said, running her hand over the circular wooden bench that wrapped itself round the tree's sturdy trunk.

'Michael helped out.'

'He's very involved in the garden,' Anne said. 'We're grateful that he lives near to us.'

'Michael and Margaret were particularly close – he struggled when she died. His way of coping was to disappear, gallivanting all over the world once he graduated.' John frowned. 'For a while, we thought he might never come back to us.'

'What changed his mind?' Vega asked.

'Time is a healer. Isn't that what they say?'

Anne said. But her voice betrayed her. Time had not healed her wounds.

'He's married now, with two kids of his own and another on the way,' John said. 'Lives five minutes' walk away. My right-hand man.'

'If you were my parents, I'd want to live nearby too,' Vega said, and John could see the sincerity on her face.

They stood side by side, leaning on the wooden railing that kept the kids safe, taking in the view.

'We used to come up quite often, but we've fallen out of the habit. I don't think I've been here in a couple of years,' Anne said. Her voice softened. 'Forth Mountain looks majestic today.' She looked to John, a question in her eyes.

He understood, nodding. It was time to share what happened to Margaret.

'You want to talk about Margaret's death, don't you?' Anne asked Vega.

'I don't want to upset either of you. It's just that while I know what happened to Margaret, I'd love to learn a little more about how it happened. In particular, who was involved and if you feel blame lies anywhere,' Vega replied.

'Do you have children?' Anne enquired.

Vega shook her head. 'I'm not ready for kids. Not sure I ever will be.'

'You'll know if and when it's the right time,' Anne said. 'John and I always knew we wanted a big family. I think we've shared enough with you to illustrate that. The four kids were close in age and best friends. But they were all so different. Mary, Margaret, Frances and Michael, each a unique individual with their own distinct personality. That's the thing you learn as a parent. You can raise children in the same home, sharing the same experiences, but they'll all grow up differently.' She paused, then added, 'React to stressful situations in completely different ways.'

John felt an ache grow in his chest. They had lived with the truth of this statement for decades. But the passage of time never dulled the pain.

'Margaret was a straight-A student. All she ever wanted was to be a doctor, but the entrance requirements for university demanded a nearly perfect Leaving Certificate,' Anne continued.

Anne glanced over to John, waiting for him to say something, but he couldn't speak. Because, even after all these years, he still blamed himself. Anne had worried and fretted about Margaret's late nights, often sharing her fears with John. But he was convinced Margaret was managing everything and Anne's worries were unnecessary.

For this, he would never forgive himself.

Anne sighed, then said flatly, 'With that kind of dedication comes stress.'

'I wrote a piece on the Leaving Certificate exams a few years ago,' Vega said. 'It horrified me how much mental stress the Irish system places on such young shoulders. The process is flawed, no doubt about it.'

'That's for sure.' Anne closed her eyes as she spoke. 'We drove to school to pick up Margaret's results together, the three of us. Friday, the twenty-sixth of August, 1992. Thirty-three years ago.' She sighed, opening her eyes again. 'Margaret rushed into the school, a bundle of nerves and excitement. If anyone deserved seven A1s, it was Margaret.'

'What did she get?' Vega asked, biting her bottom lip.

'Five A1s and two A2s.'

'That's still an incredible result,' Vega said.

'Yes, she was one of the top students at her school, and we were so proud of her. But Margaret was gutted, because she knew it wasn't good enough for medical school,' John said.

'We told her how proud we were,' Anne insisted. 'She could reapply and re-sit again. But she wouldn't discuss it with us, just clammed up and refused to talk about her options. Which was not like her, because she always talked to me. But, no matter how hard I tried, I couldn't get her to open up this time.'

Watching his wife in pain as she relived that horrific day was unbearable. John wanted to escape, to run away from this chapter of their life story. But he had learned that no matter where he ran, the pain always followed him.

Anne wrapped her arms round herself as she continued to recount their nightmare. 'We were relieved when she told us she was going out with her friends as planned to a nightclub in Wexford. If she had a drink, let her hair down, she'd gain some perspective. Her friends would help her see things differently. John drove her into town, gave her some money, and told her to call for a lift home . . .' Anne's voice broke, and she began to cry softly. 'I'm sorry . . . I can't . . .'

Vega placed a hand on Anne's shoulder. 'You don't have to continue. We can stop.'

Anne looked up to John, her eyes pleading with him to take over. He cleared his throat and pressed on. 'The phone rang earlier than we expected. We were in the sitting room, watching *Prime Time*. It was Margaret's best friend, Lorna, and she was hysterical. Margaret was on her way to Wexford Hospital in an ambulance.

We left immediately, but by the time we arrived...'

Silence filled the air on that wooden platform. The birdsong, which earlier had sounded joyful, now became a mournful hymn.

Vega remained silent. No clichéd 'I'm sorry', just the quiet respect that the horror of their loss warranted.

Anne moved to John's side, and they swayed into each other, offering strength once more, until their tears subsided.

'Did the doctors confirm how she died?' Vega asked softly when they pulled apart.

John noted the tears in Vega's eyes, and he smiled sadly at her. She was a kind girl. 'The doctors said that she'd taken ecstasy and that, in the hot environment of the club, combined with alcohol, Margaret had a heart attack. It's rare. But it can happen,' John said.

'Had Margaret taken drugs before?' Vega asked.

'Her friends all swore, and we believed them, that none of them had dabbled. When they saw Margaret talking to a well-known drug dealer in the club, they were worried,' John said.

Vega stood up and walked towards them both, her brow furrowed in a frown. 'Can I ask if his name was Hinges?'

John looked at her sharply. Anne was right: Vega *was* chasing the Hinges element. Damn it! 'How do you know that?'

'I've come across him in my research on the drug crisis in the area,' Vega replied. 'And the Grants told me that they met you when you went to court during Hinges's manslaughter trial. I put two and two together . . .'

John clenched his fists, his body tensing at the mention of that man's name.

Then Anne spoke for them both, her voice strong and clear, 'Hinges murdered our daughter.'

Twelve

Anne

25 August 1998

All Anne wanted was for Hinges to admit what he had done. His denial of his crime felt like a denial of her daughter – a further insult and blow.

'Friday, twenty-sixth of August 1992,' Anne said, her voice ice cold.

Hinges whipped his head round to look at her. 'What about it?'

'You were in the Havana Club in Wexford.'

'Was I? If you say so,' Hinges replied, watching Anne uncertainly, unsure where she was headed.

'The Leaving Cert results came out that day,' Anne continued, her heart rate quickening as memories assaulted her.

Watching Margaret run inside her school entrance, nervously clutching her best friend

Lorna's arm. Waiting in the car, expecting to see Margaret's big smile that could brighten any room. Margaret finally emerging from the school, her head bowed, tears streaking her red cheeks. Five years of study notes, and late nights revising, and a lifelong dream, shattered.

Anne saw Hinge's eyes narrow as he watched tears fall down her face. She wiped them away furiously, turning to John to continue. She would not allow that man to see her grief.

'You all right?' John whispered as she moved past him to the corner of the room. She squeezed his hand in reassurance, then moved out of Hinges's line of sight, grabbing a tea-towel to wipe her tears away.

John pulled a chair in close to Hinges. 'Margaret was seventeen years old. Our second eldest. And when she didn't get the results she wanted, she was vulnerable.'

'Look, man, shit happens,' Hinges said. 'I didn't even pass my intermediate certificate. Didn't do me no harm.'

'Yeah, sure. *No harm to you!* But the same can't be said for the kids who fall into your path, *can it?*' John yelled, his face suddenly red as he stood up and pushed his chair back so hard it fell to the side.

Seeing John's anger put a fire into Anne too.

She threw the tea towel to the ground and raced to Hinges's side. 'You gave our daughter ecstasy! A freebie. To take the edge off. *That's what you told her!*' she screamed. Her hands balled into fists and she pummelled his chest. *'You murdered our child!'*

Anne felt John's arms pulling her back, away from Hinges, his voice whispering, 'Easy now.'

But there was no easy any more.

She wanted to pound on his chest until Hinges called out in pain.

Until he begged her to stop.

She wanted to use her bare hands to claw his eyes out.

She wanted him dead.

She pulled against John's arms, which held her close and heard a laugh from Hinges that stopped them both in their tracks.

'You need to put a leash on your woman,' Hinges said, mocking Anne, mocking them both.

John released Anne and moved closer to Hinges, leaning in low until he was nose to nose with the man, and growled, 'One more word about my wife, and I'll knock you into next week.'

Hinges shrugged, a smirk lingering on his face. If he was affected by the events of the day, he didn't show it.

'How many kids have you murdered?' John asked. 'We know two for sure – our Margaret and Stephen Grant.'

'I was acquitted of that. Nothing to do with me,' Hinges replied, the smirk growing wider by the second.

'You're a monster!' Anne shouted. 'You killed that kid, you killed Margaret and goodness knows how many others. Last week, another local teen died from an overdose, reported in the *Wexford People*. Did you sell him the drugs that finished him? Or perhaps you were the one who started him off on his journey to addiction? Gave him his first taste as a freebie. Like you did with Margaret!'

'Prove it,' Hinges replied, all trace of mirth now gone and a cold edge to his voice. 'I'm getting sick of these games. Untie me, and let me go, before you both live to regret it.'

John motioned to Anne, nodding towards the hall. He wanted to talk.

'I'm curious. What's your end game? Cos from where I stand –' Hinges laughed – 'or should I say *sit*, you don't have any idea what to do next.' He caught John's eye, then continued. 'My guess is your missus surprised you with this. And now you need to clean up her mess. Tell you what, pal, let me go, and I'll let this go. But if I'm not out that door in less than five minutes you've got a problem.'

'You don't get to make demands!' Anne screamed.

'No, you don't,' John agreed. 'And if you don't shut up I'm gagging you again.

John and Anne walked out to the hall, closing the door behind them.

John sighed. 'We have to let him go.'

'What?' Anne was gobsmacked. 'Not yet. We can't let him out. Not now, not with the results out tomorrow. Not without accepting responsibility.'

'He's never going to give you what you need. He can't show remorse because he doesn't give a damn about what he's done.'

Anne heard the truth in that statement.

'Plus, as I said earlier, anything he's said here wouldn't be admissible in court, even if the Gardaí arrested him,' John added.

Anne felt nauseous. For the first time, she began to doubt her actions. 'We can't let him go. It will all have been for nothing.'

'We have to,' John said. 'But not for nothing. We'll tell him that we'll keep the video of him confessing to dealing drugs, and we won't release it, as long as he walks away and leaves Wexford.'

'He'll move on to another place and start dealing there,' Anne protested.

'There's nothing we can do about that. We're not vigilantes. We're Anne and John, a middle-aged couple who have lost one of the most precious things in their lives.' He locked eyes with Anne, 'But we are in danger of losing everything else if we don't stop this now.'

Anne nodded, feeling her body sag with regret.

John's voice softened. 'I get it, Anne. I want to smash his head in, make him feel the pain that we both do. But that's not who we are. I want to go back to us. Let's call the girls and ask them to visit this weekend. Try to get hold of Michael too. We can fire up the barbecue. Enjoy each other again. Make a new memory. I can't keep doing this . . . It's killing me. It's killing us.'

Anne took a deep breath and felt something change within her. Her husband's words struck her hard, and she recognised their truth. If she kept going down this way, they wouldn't survive. She clasped John's hand, and together they walked back into the room.

Thirteen

Vega

7 April 2025

Hearing Anne confirm that Hinges was responsible for Margaret's death was not a surprise. This man, whom she'd been trying to locate for weeks now, had caused so much trauma. Was he lying on a beach in Spain, living his best life, totally oblivious to the pain and destruction he'd left in his wake? Or on a new patch, in another town in Ireland, giving freebies to a new batch of kids?

'I can't imagine what you've been through,' Vega said, her voice a little shaky. They'd got to her, this lovely couple.

'I hope you never have to experience it,' Anne said.

'I haven't lost a child, but I have lost people in my life.' Vega stood up, and her eyes took in the garden from this perfect vantage point. Every tree was a monument to the Davis family. She turned back to the couple, who were still arm in arm. 'Did you ever confront Hinges?'

John and Anne exchanged a look.

What was that? A look of warning passed from one to the other? Or was Vega's mind in overdrive, as it often was?

'Yes. Twice,' Anne replied, as John said, 'Once.'

Interesting, Vega thought.

'You said you've spoken to the Grants about the court case in 1998? After their son Stephen overdosed on MDMA bought at the Havana nightclub?' John interjected quickly.

'Yes.'

'Anne and I went to Hinges's trial every day, thinking we would witness the man who murdered our daughter get his punishment. The club's management had installed CCTV, but hadn't informed the public. And the footage clearly showed Hinges on camera, huddled in a corner with Stephen Grant, selling him drugs,' John said.

Anne cut in, 'If you saw the way he strutted in every day, like he owned the place – a bloody smirk on his face, completely uncaring of the Grant family. Stephen's poor mother cried every day of the trial. We became friendly with them – you'd be surprised how much time is spent outside the courtroom, waiting for the proceedings to begin or continue.'

'Elaine Grant said you'd been a huge comfort to her,' Vega said.

Anne shrugged. 'Nobody understands a parent's heartbreak better than another heartbroken parent.'

'We had our chance to confront him on the second day of trial. We arrived at the courthouse at the same time as him,' John said.

Anne's voice turned cold as she remembered the encounter. 'I told him that Margaret Davis was our daughter. That she died from an overdose of ecstasy, bought from him six years earlier.'

'How did he react?'

'He rolled his eyes, and carried on walking,' John said, his jaw clenched and eyes ice-cold.

Vega sighed, remembering the details of the case. The video footage became the crux of both the defence and prosecution, and ultimately got Hinges off. The prosecution insisted it showed Hinges in conversation with Stephen, heads bent low. The defence used the footage to create a reasonable doubt because the camera's timestamp was set to the wrong date and time, thus throwing its accuracy into jeopardy.

'It must have been difficult to watch him walk free,' Vega said.

'Hearing that monster get off scot-free, and the heart-wrenching cries of Stephen's family will never leave me,' John said.

'He took away much more than Margaret,' Anne added. 'He changed every one of us. The girls and Michael rarely left their bedrooms for a year after she died. And now they carry their grief every day, like we do. That was all on Hinges.'

Was on Hinges, not *is* on Hinges, Vega thought. Interesting that Anne used the past tense.

'If he'd shown some remorse even, it might have been bearable,' John said.

'You said you confronted him twice,' Vega said, turning to Anne.

John threw another warning look. This time, Vega was one hundred per cent certain of it.

'Did I? It was once,' Anne said, shrugging. 'Let's go down the slide.'

'I'm not sure that's a good idea,' John said. 'Would the ladder be safer?'

'I disagree. It's an excellent idea. But tell you what, you can go first. Go on . . .' She pushed him towards the slide and laughed happily when he obliged and whooshed down. Anne went next, where John waited to catch her at the end. Then Vega swung her legs over and on to the slide, landing in an undignified heap on the grass.

They began to make their way towards the final bench in the garden. John up front, and Anne falling into step again with Vega.

'The maze is a beautiful memorial to Margaret,' Vega said. 'It's an extraordinary feat. Did you begin building it straight away after she died or later on?'

'Later. The twenty-eighth of August, 1998,' Anne replied.

'Wow, you remember the exact date again!' Vega said, looking at Anne in surprise.

John stopped dead in his tracks in front of them and turned round. 'We'd spent a long time considering ways to honour Margaret. When we decided to plant the blossom tree, it was a special moment.'

Somehow that statement seemed untrue. And why did Vega have a nagging feeling about that date? It felt like a loose thread was hanging in front of her, but she couldn't quite grasp it with her fingers.

Fourteen

John

25 August 1998

It was time to make Hinges believe a deal could be brokered.

'Well?' Hinges asked, his bushy brown eyebrows raised in question.

'You murdered our daughter,' John said evenly.

'So you said. But, as I told you already, I didn't kill her. The drugs did. That's not on me. It's on her for taking them,' Hinges replied.

'You don't feel any remorse, do you?' John said.

Hinges's eyes narrowed as he replied, 'Look, I'm sorry your kid died. That must suck. But if you blame me then you might as well blame the cartel I buy the drugs from. I'm a small part of a much bigger wheel.'

At last, John thought – something he could use.

'Who do you buy from, then? Europe? Or further afield? The Mexicans?'

'A cartel in Dublin, who bring them in from Spain. You gonna kidnap all them too?'

'No. I don't suppose I can,' John said. 'I'll let you go, but there are conditions.'

'Go on,' Hinges replied warily.

'First, you need to stop selling drugs. Second, you have to leave Wexford.'

Hinges scoffed at the mere suggestion.

'Third, you need to agree that you will not retaliate in any form for tonight,' John said.

'Or what? You're gonna kill me?' Hinges said. 'You ain't no killer, and neither is your mad missus.'

'You're right – we're no killers – but what you don't realise is that we've been recording all of this.'

Anne walked over to the dresser at the back of the kitchen and moved the cookbook to reveal the hidden camcorder. Then she said sweetly, 'Smile. You're on Candid Camera.'

The smirk left Hinges's face.

'You've said on camera not only that you deal drugs, but where the supply chain originates from. I suspect the Gardaí would find this interesting. But, more than that, I reckon your pals in the cartel wouldn't be happy at how chatty you are. So maybe we don't bother giving it to the Gardaí, but instead release it to the media. Let them do what they want with it.'

John felt a moment of triumph when he saw how quiet Hinges had become.

'As I said, agree to my terms and I'll release you. But not before I put this tape somewhere safe, with the instruction that if anything happens to me or my wife it will be sent to a friend, who happens to be a journalist.'

This was a bluff, but the flash of fear on Hinges's face showed he'd fallen for it. Anne beamed at John in approval.

'I need to think about this,' Hinges said.

'Take your time,' John replied.

'I'd need a few weeks to sort my shit out,' Hinges said.

'You can have one week,' John replied.

'Give me a drink of water, will ya?' Hinges asked.

'Sure, we can do that,' Anne replied, refilling the paper cup. She moved over to Hinges and leaned down to place the cup to his lips.

As Hinges thought about their offer, John began to formulate a plan. He'd take the tape to the office safe, then return to drive Hinges to his house. Hopefully, the threat of exposure and the messiness of the tape being released to the media would be a deterrent for him.

'I've been thinking about relocating to Spain as it happens,' Hinges said. 'So all right. Let me go, and you'll never see me again.'

Fifteen

Anne

Once the decision was made, everything unfolded swiftly, as John planned. When they dropped him off at the end of his lane, they'd half expected Hinges to lunge at them, but other than shouting a few expletives he hurried towards his house.

They drove home in silence. When they got in, Anne prepared a tray with the promised casserole so they could eat on their laps while watching TV. They'd missed the news unfortunately, but maybe that was a good thing, as they'd had enough excitement for one night. They called the girls and asked them to come home at the weekend. Mary and Frances were unsure at first, saying they had plans, but eventually agreed when they heard their parents' excitement at renewing their tradition of a yearly barbecue.

Michael didn't answer their call. Voicemail

was the closest they got to him these days. But they'd left a heartfelt message, pleading with him to give them another chance. The family needed him. And they believed he needed them too. Anne didn't hold much hope, but perhaps, soon, he'd realise that they all could be together without it being too painful.

Anne and John decided they'd prepare a feast – they'd put music on, and make sure that the weekend was full of laughter and love. They'd find a way to create new memories.

The following morning, John woke Anne with a loving kiss. His face was bright, his eyes shining. 'I had the nicest dream last night. We were all at Powerscourt.'

'The Japanese garden,' Anne said, smiling.

'Yes. And it was simply beautiful, watching Margaret walk down the aisle with blossoms in her hair. And when I woke up I knew what we should do!'

'What, my love?'

'We need to buy a cherry-blossom tree and plant it in her honour.'

'A tree for Margaret. Oh, I love that idea. Where will we plant it?'

'I'm not sure. Somewhere in our garden, pride of place, so we can look at it every day and remember her. I'll go down to the garden centre to buy one.'

Anne reached over and pulled John towards her to plant a kiss on his lips. 'Buy a mature tree. Don't take any chances on a young tree that might break in a storm.'

'No expense spared!' John agreed with a smile. 'We can show the girls when they come down in the morning.'

'While you do that, I'll start working on what we'll need for the barbecue. I'll make a list!' She made a sheepish face, thinking of the list she'd shown him the day before. It all felt so silly now. What had she been thinking? Taking on a drug dealer. Her? Her mouth started to twitch. 'Can you imagine Mary and Frances's faces, if you told them what I'd done? They'd never believe it!' Anne spluttered out.

'Stop!' John said, shaking his head. 'We can never tell anyone!'

Anne might not have had the outcome she'd hoped she would yesterday, but somehow it had helped all the same. She felt changed by the encounter. Stronger.

After breakfast, John left for the garden centre and Anne turned her attention to cleaning. She started by changing all the bed linen in the bedrooms, dusting the dressers and mirrors. Then, satisfied that it looked perfect, she decided that a cup of coffee would do nicely as she began making her list for the weekend's groceries.

Singing softly, she walked into the kitchen.

But a hand grabbed her roughly, and before she realised what was happening she was in a headlock, unable to move.

She smelled him before she saw him.

Hinges was back.

Sixteen

Anne

7 April 2025

Almost twenty-eight years had passed since they'd planted that first tree, and now it was unrecognisable. It had flourished, growing stronger each year; its roots deep into the ground. Now, it stood nearly seven metres high, and this year its double pink cherry blossoms cascaded over a dark and fissured bark.

'The blossoms look like a fountain,' Vega said.

'This is our only weeping kiku cherry tree. We call it Margaret's tree, because we planted it for her.' Anne's voice quivered with emotion.

And beneath the low branches was the fourth wooden slatted bench – two metres long, with its grain stained to a rich dark brown.

'The last bench,' Vega said.

'Well, yes, but also the first. This was where the garden started.'

'In 1998,' Vega repeated. 'When you planted this first tree, in memory of Margaret, did you envision it growing to all of this?'

'No.' Anne looked at John, and years seemed to melt away as they returned to that fateful August. 'The idea for the garden came afterwards.'

John's eyes widened, and Anne realised she'd misspoken.

Vega, of course, missed nothing. 'I thought you said you remembered the exact date of the garden's inception because you had put so much thought into it.'

John came to the rescue once more, closing ranks. 'We did spend months trying to think of ways to honour Margaret. The idea of a tree came to me, after a dream I had about our visit to Powerscourt. The maze as it is, came later.'

'Oh, I see,' Vega replied, but her eyes remained thoughtful as she watched them both.

Anne felt her hackles rise. They'd done nothing wrong. Well, that wasn't quite right. They'd done nothing that she was ashamed of.

'Has it helped?' Vega asked, changing tack.

'It has,' Anne replied instantly. 'We've had so much pleasure in this garden, adding to it, watching it evolve and change with each season. Before the maze, there were days when it was hard to find a reason to get out of bed.'

John looked down at the grassy ground, as if the mere mention of those darker days were enough to send him back again.

'Once the kids left for college, it was just the two of us. John would go to work, and I'd be here alone, with my thoughts, which were always on Margaret. I was angry. I was so bloody angry.'

'And you?' Vega asked John. 'Were you angry?'

'Why wouldn't I be? I'd not only lost my daughter but also my wife and children to their grief. And who wanted to be here? A house full of sorrow.'

Vega approached the tree and ran her fingertips over the bark. 'Tell me how the garden changed that.'

John joined her side and crouched down, touching the ground around the wide trunk. 'I dug the hole for this tree myself. And with every inch of ground I lifted with my spade, I felt a little of my anger melt away.'

'And when we placed the tree into the hole, and began filling it again with soil, it was the same for me too. As the earth swallowed up the roots of the tree, it seemed to swallow up my anger too. A great weight lifted from my shoulders in that moment,' Anne added.

'Anne suggested we plant the tree here, rather

than in our back garden, and she was right, as always.'

Anne beamed. She appreciated it when he acknowledged this fact. 'But it was John who turned it into this.'

'The tree looked a little lost on its own. I felt it could do with some company, which turned into this,' John said with his customary shrug.

'How many trees did you say you'd planted?' Vega asked.

'There are about two hundred in total. But we received some donations too. Our families bought some trees from the local garden centre,' John said.

'Then some friends of Margaret's called round and asked if they could donate a tree too. It developed a life of its own,' Anne added.

'Do you remember that first spring morning?' John asked.

Of course she did. Her eyes sparkled. 'I couldn't sleep. I woke up at five a.m., nearly two hours before the alarm. This fellow was passed out cold beside me,' Anne said, nudging John in the ribs. 'I got a notion to go up to the garden, in my slippers and dressing gown, with a cup of tea, to say good morning to Margaret. I'd got into a habit of chatting to her up there. And I've never seen anything like it. Overnight, every bud blossomed, and our beautiful green top field had transformed into a stunning display of cherry pinks and apple whites. It took my breath away.'

'I found her sitting on the damp ground, amid the dew, sobbing and laughing, with the birdsong as her backing track,' John said.

'Happy tears. I'd never felt more connected to Margaret since she'd died. It's how we like to think of her. Running around the cherry blossoms in Powerscourt, smiling and carefree, so happy. That's where her heaven is. And ours too one day when we leave this world.'

Vega wiped tears from her cheeks with the back of her hand.

Anne gave her arm a gentle squeeze. She was a good girl.

'I began making the bench that evening after work. I knew I needed somewhere for Anne to sit each day,' John added.

'And the most wonderful thing of all happened: the kids started to come home again. We were giddy,' Anne said.

'And your son?' Vega asked.

'He moved back in again! He's been helping his dad transform the maze ever since his return,' Anne said, smiling proudly.

'He met a local girl, and they got married in

2012. They'll be along once the kids get home from school. He's here most days.'

'And you've raised so much money for charity,' Vega said.

'Our eldest daughter, Mary, suggested that. She's a clever one and saw the potential before we did. Cherry blossom is called sakura in Japan – millions go to see the ornamental blossoms in Japan every spring. Causes quite the frenzy. So Mary said why don't we open the maze up to the public at weekends, and place a donation bucket at the gate, allowing people to give what they can,' Anne said.

'I think you might be the nicest couple I've met,' Vega said, making Anne blush. 'And, also, you must have the greenest fingers! I can't keep a plant alive, but every single tree has flourished for you. Especially this one, the first. It looks like it's been here since time began.'

'It's in the preparation,' John said, clearing his throat. 'You have to dig a perfect hole, making sure there is enough space for the roots to spread.'

'And make sure you improve the soil with organic matter too, to help keep it fertile,' Anne added seriously, a brief smile flickering when she saw John's mouth twitch in response.

'I appreciate you both taking the time to

speak with me. Thank you,' Vega said. She closed her notebook. 'I've got more than enough for my story. Can I call you if I think of anything else?'

'Of course. You are welcome any time,' Anne said sincerely. 'Would you like tea before you go? Can I tempt you with cake?'

'No, thank you. I'm going to get home and write this while it's all fresh in my head. No need to get up – I can make my own way to the car.' Vega walked over to John and shook his hand, then turned to do the same to Anne.

But Anne got up from the bench and instead gave Vega a warm hug. As Vega left the garden, disappearing beneath the blossom canopy, Anne sat back down on the bench beside John, exhaling in relief. They'd done the interview. And it couldn't have gone better.

Trouble had not met them on the road this time.

Seventeen

Vega

Once Vega settled into her car, she felt an overwhelming urge to talk to her boyfriend, Luka. She was unsettled, and she couldn't quite understand why. But Luka always seemed to centre her. She sent him a message asking if he could talk. As a social worker, he didn't always have access to his phone. And she knew that this morning, he was rehoming two brothers into foster care.

His response was to video call immediately.

'How did this morning go?' Vega enquired.

'Perfectly. The foster couple are farmers, and the lads' eyes lit up when they saw the amount of land that is now their playground.'

'I'm so happy they got to stay together,' Vega said, feeling a lump in her throat.

'How did it go at the maze?'

'Great. Anne and John met when they were children and have been together for sixty years. The way they take care of each other is sweet.'

'It's a beautiful thing, to find someone to grow old with.'

'Yes,' Vega replied huskily. They exchanged a smile, an unspoken question and answer moving between them. 'You did it again.'

'What?'

'Made me feel better,' Vega said.

'I'm glad about that. But what's up?' Luka asked, his forehead furrowing into a frown.

'I feel like I'm missing something here,' she replied with a sigh, 'You know that drug dealer I've been trying to track down?'

'Yer man Hinges, who got off in that murder trial?'

'Yes, him, well, he's the man who supplied Anne and John's daughter with drugs. I don't think they'll ever get over her death.'

'That's understandable. So do they know where this Hinges bloke is?'

'They said they didn't. But something doesn't feel quite right, although I can't quite figure out what it is. It's like loose threads are dangling in front of me . . .'

'He's probably dead,' Luka said. When Vega raised an eyebrow in question, he continued, 'Look, guys like Hinges are either on the run from a drug cartel or the Gardaí.' Then he added ominously, 'Or in a shallow grave somewhere.'

The hairs on Vega's arms stood up, and she gasped aloud as loose threads began to knit together, one by one. 'Luka, sorry, I've got to go. Love you.'

She picked up her notebook and flipped back through pages of notes until she found what she was searching for, hoping that she was mistaken.

'Damn it, Anne and John,' she whispered, her suspicions confirmed with one damning detail.

Eighteen

Anne

26 August 1998

Anne struggled against Hinges, but was powerless to move.

'Doesn't feel so good when it's your turn now, does it?' he growled into her ear.

'What do you want?' she asked.

'Where's your husband?' Hinges asked.

'He's out,' Anne said, and had never felt such relief from a fact in her life. She'd brought this crazy man to their door, so it was her and only her who should pay the price.

But then she heard the slam of a car door, and John's face came into view through the glass in the back door. She tried to shout a warning, but Hinges pressed a sweaty hand over her mouth, holding it firmly.

'Wait till you see the beauty I bought,' John said, walking into the kitchen. The smile on his face froze in horror when he saw Anne's situation.

It only took John seconds to react, but as soon as he moved forward Hinges tightened his grip and said, 'I'll snap her neck if you walk one inch closer.'

'Let her go,' John demanded. 'If you hurt her, if you harm one hair on her head . . .'

Hinges squeezed his arms tighter, and for the first time Anne cried out in pain. Her eyes locked with John's in panic.

'Give me the videotape,' Hinges said.

'It's not here. As I told you, it's somewhere safe. If you hurt Anne or me, it will go to a journalist,' John said evenly.

'Maybe I don't care. It would be worth the fallout to see you two go down.'

There was no point in reasoning with this man. Anne would have to talk to Hinges in a language he understood. She swung her arm slamming Hinges in the groin, but didn't connect, and he pulled back his fist and punched her across the side of her head, sending her flailing to the ground. His eyes scanned the room, and he ran towards the kitchen counter by the AGA stove, reaching for the block of kitchen knives.

He picked up the largest butcher's blade and rushed towards John.

Dazed, Anne started to move towards her husband, who was trying to hold off Hinges from plunging the knife into his chest.

And then the back door opened.

Michael.

Was she dreaming?

She watched her son rush towards his father and leap on to Hinges's back. They all toppled to the ground in one crashing heap. Anne crawled towards them, terror filling every part of her, as they tussled on the floor, Michael fighting to gain control of the knife that Hinges was now aiming in his direction.

John moved first of all, rolling to his right. He yanked Hinges off Michael, who lay motionless underneath him.

'Michael!' Anne screamed, when she saw blood pool into a puddle on her shiny white floor tiles.

'He ... didn't ... get me,' Michael said, his voice shaking with shock.

Anne scrambled towards Michael and John on all fours, prepared to stand between them and Hinges. Ready to fight.

But Hinges didn't move.

Hinges would never move again.

Nineteen

John

26 August 1998

'He's dead,' John said, moving his hand away from Hinge's non-existent pulse.

Anne and Michael rocked together on the floor a couple of metres away.

'I can't believe you're here,' Anne whispered.

'I was at the girls' flat when you called last night. I've been back in Ireland for a few days. I borrowed a friend's car, decided to surprise you,' Michael said, his voice still trembling. He stood up, then reached down to offer his mother a hand. 'What the hell is that man doing in our kitchen?' he asked.

'You need to leave here,' John said, trying to push him towards the door.

'Are you kidding me? I'm not going anywhere,' Michael stated firmly. 'Thank God I arrived when I did! He would have killed you, Dad. You too, Mam. He's a madman, coming here to attack you. We need to call the Gardaí.'

Anne and John exchanged a worried look.

'There's a little more to this,' Anne said.

John placed an arm round Anne's trembling shoulders as she filled in an astonished Michael on the events of the previous day.

'Jesus, Mam,' Michael said, shaking his head in disbelief, his face white with shock. He moved closer and looked down at Hinges's body. 'If you knew how many times I dreamed of killing him . . .'

'You can't say that to the Gardaí!' Anne said in horror.

'I killed him – not you. You didn't do this, son,' John stated firmly.

'No, Dad. I twisted his arm round and pushed the knife into him,' Michael argued.

'That was self-defence – either way, I won't let you or your dad take the blame for this,' Anne said tearfully. 'This is on me. I lured him here. I killed him. Both of you need to leave. I'll call the Gardaí to confess.'

Both John and Michael gave Anne a look that clearly showed her suggestion wasn't open to discussion.

John stood up, pacing the floor as he ran through the scenarios open to them. 'If we call the Gardaí and tell them Hinges called here out of the blue to attack us, the full story would come out – Anne's plan, her buying the chloroform. Nobody will believe us that it was self-defence. They will say it's premeditated.'

'That's why I have to confess,' Anne repeated tearfully.

'No!' both John and Michael said at once.

An hour passed as the three of them went round in circles, trying to work out their next move. Each was willing to take the blame to save the others, but none of them was willing to allow it.

'I've lost one daughter because of that man. I'll be damned if I'll let him take one more thing from me,' John said eventually, his face drawn and pale. 'We can't report this. We have to bury the body.'

Anne and Michael nodded their consent solemnly.

'But you can't be here for that,' John said to Michael. 'Go back to Dublin. Tell the girls you will come home tomorrow with them.'

Michael held a hand up, ready to argue.

'I mean it, Michael,' John stated firmly. 'I won't have any discussion on this. I'll take care of the body and, if this comes back on us, so be it. But I will not allow this to come back on you.'

Anne was sobbing now, the shock wearing off and in its place horror flooding in. 'Please, Michael. Do as your dad says.'

Eventually Michael reluctantly agreed. Before he left, he hugged each of them tightly. And he held on to John for longer than he had done since he was a little boy.

'I'm not sorry, Dad,' Michael whispered into his embrace. 'He would have killed you both.'

'I know, son.' John clapped his back and drew him in closer.

'I want to stay.'

'I know that too. But one day, when you have children of your own, you'll understand why I've made you leave.'

Once Michael was on his way, John put Hinges back into the wheelbarrow.

'We'll not bury him in our garden – he needs to go into the top field,' Anne said.

Together, they moved Hinges's body. Then John started to dig on what would be the hottest day of the summer of 1998.

By the time John had broken the soil and started to make some headway into the dry, packed dirt, the sun was beating down on his back. A river of sweat travelled from the nape of his neck down his back. His T-shirt was plastered to his body.

'Let me help,' Anne pleaded for the third time.

He shook his head, refusing to stop and answer her. They had been through this before. Her back had always been a vulnerability for her, and he would be damned if he let Hinges cause her any more pain. Besides, John needed to do this. With each strike into the soil, John thought of Margaret, of the day she was born, tiny, a scrap of a thing weighing five pounds six ounces. He'd been worried ever since Anne had discovered she was pregnant. It was too soon after their firstborn, Mary, who was only three months old. Irish twins. They were barely making ends meet, both exhausted from work and parenting. In Wexford Hospital, after twelve long hours of labour, Anne handed Margaret to him, fear shadowing her eyes, unsure whether he would love his second child as much as his first, whether he had room for another person in his heart.

But he need never have worried, because when Margaret's little hand clung to John'pinkie, all his doubts and worries vanished. As Anne always said, he was wrapped round Margaret's little finger. And what a wonderful place that was to be.

Love filled him as more memories flooded him. Watching her receive the sacrament on her

First Holy Communion, wearing a long white dress with a lace veil. She swaggered towards them, making a face as she tasted the holy bread for the first time, Anne and John stifling a laugh. Then as Margaret sat back down between her parents on the church pew, John had a vision that took his breath away.

He saw Margaret, a young woman, again in a long white dress with a lace veil, walking down the church aisle on his arm to her beloved.

But, of course, there would be no white wedding for Margaret.

John felt a hand graze his shoulder, bringing him back from his memory, which could cause him so much joy and sorrow, all at once.

'That's enough, John. You can stop digging now,' Anne said. And her eyes glistened in understanding. Without any need for explanation, she understood what her husband was going through, because his pain was her pain too.

John pulled his T-shirt off and over his shoulders, using it to wipe the sweat and tears from his face. Then he looked around himself in amazement at the deep hole he'd created and was now standing in. It was nearly as tall as he was, at least six feet.

John heaved himself out of the hole and walked over to the wheelbarrow that sat a couple of metres away. A tarp that usually covered the patio set in the evenings was now draped over a body.

How had they come to this?

'Are you sure?' Anne asked. 'We can still call the Gardaí and I'll confess.'

John's answer was to wheel the barrow towards the hole and tip it over.

Hinges landed with a dull thud.

He started refilling the hole with soil, quickly covering the body. Then, once John had filled the hole half a metre high, he added a bag of compost. Anne dragged the six-foot blossom tree towards him, and he placed it into the hole before shovelling the earth back in.

Until at last it was over.

He felt Anne's arms wrap round his body from behind, and she rested her head on his back. He leaned into the embrace and closed his eyes, absorbing her love and support, her strength.

'He did this to himself,' Anne said.

John knew this was partly true. But they were not without blame.

He'd spent a lifetime as a peacemaker, lover and friend. He'd never raised his voice to anyone and was known for his gentle nature – until that moment when he'd seen his wife vulnerable, when anger had sparked through every part of him.

Even the most mild-tempered people could break.

Twenty

Anne

7 April 2025

Anne and John sat in silence beneath the blossom tree, listening to the birdsong and the rustling leaves in the breeze. Their spontaneous burst of laughter had been the release they both desperately needed from the stress of the interview.

'I think we might be close to peak blossom day. This weekend will be a busy one. I suspect we'll have a lot around,' John said. 'I need to look at that gate. It's a little stiff.'

Anne fidgeted on the bench, a twinge in her back niggling her. 'I think I might have pulled something when I went down that slide.'

John turned to her, frustration visible on his handsome face. 'I knew that was a bad idea! You're not twenty-one any more, Anne.'

Anne smiled, leaning in to kiss him on the

lips. 'Oh, maybe not on the outside. But in here –' she touched her head and heart – 'I'm still that young woman. Bad back or not, it was worth it. Felt good to be whizzing down, wind in my hair.'

'What will I do with you?' John replied grumpily, but she could tell he was itching to smile. 'You go inside and put your feet up for the rest of the day. I'll cook tonight.'

Anne laughed. 'When you say cook, you mean—'

'A chippy tea!'

Anne licked her lips. 'Fish and chips, lots of salt and vinegar. Mushy peas! We'll worry about the cholesterol tomorrow.'

'Deal,' John said. 'Will we go inside? I'll make us that pot of tea we've been promising ourselves.'

'A few more minutes. I'm not ready to go in yet.' She leaned her head on his shoulder. 'I've been worrying again about whether we should tell the girls about the garden?'

John considered her question for a few moments, and she let him be, giving him time to think through all angles. It was a topic they'd debated many times over the years, and in the end they decided to keep their secret, but with safeguards.

'Nothing has changed, as far as I'm concerned. It's been a burden for us to carry this. We don't have the right to put it on the girls' shoulders. Bad enough that Michael has to live with it. We say nothing.'

Anne nodded. She agreed with him as it went, but talking with Vega today stirred up a lot of emotions and fears. 'I know you're right. And they'll respect our wishes that the maze remains in the family, as a memorial garden for Margaret.'

'Exactly. Michael spends more time here tending the trees now than I do. He's the next caretaker when we can't do it any longer. And he's promised to ensure he appoints one of the grandchildren to take over from him when the time comes.'

'He's a good kid,' Anne repeated. 'They all are.'

'Some kids!' John joked. 'All grown up with children of their own . . .'

'They'll always be kids to us.' Anne cuddled into John again.

A sudden movement to their left made them start, and they turned in surprise to see Vega standing a few metres away from them.

'Did you forget something?' Anne asked, smiling as she sat upright.

'The date!' Vega exclaimed, moving towards

them. Two dots of pink flushed her cheeks, and her eyes sparkled.

Anne and John exchanged a puzzled glance.

'The date you started this garden. Twenty-eighth of August 1998, you said.'

'Yes,' Anne answered.

'I told you that I thought it was odd that you remembered the exact date,' Vega went on.

'And I told you that when you are planting a tree in memory of your dead daughter, you tend to remember the details,' John replied in a low voice.

Vega took another step closer. 'When I started this story and began searching for Hinges, it was the strangest thing. Nobody seemed to notice that he had even gone missing. He has no siblings, and his parents are dead. No friends that I could find. It was as if he vanished into thin air and nobody cared.'

'You get what you give in life,' Anne replied, irritation edging into her voice.

'But he had an on/off girlfriend. Julie is a recovered addict who only hooked up with Hinges because he gave her drugs. Even so, she was still annoyed that he'd stood her up and ghosted her.'

'It happens,' John said.

'The thing is, she remembered the exact

date because it was her birthday – would you believe it was the twenty-eighth of August?' Vega said.

Silence settled over the blossom maze as Vega's eyes flitted between Anne and John.

John squeezed Anne's arm more firmly this time, clearly silently conveying a message.

Let me do the talking.

But there was no way she would let him take the blame for this. If Vega had worked out their secret, she alone would hold her hands up.

'That's a coincidence,' John said evenly to Vega.

'A pretty big coincidence,' Vega replied. 'What happened to Hinges?'

'How would we know?' John replied, standing up now and facing Vega squarely.

'He's dead,' Anne said, joining his side. And when John groaned she added, 'That is, I suspect he is.'

Vega's face paled, her notebook and pencil in hand. She was clearly wrestling with what to do with what she thought she knew, Anne guessed.

'And if Hinges is dead then I'd also say that was a good thing,' Anne added.

'Go on,' Vega said.

'Because if his dying meant that one parent

did not have to endure the heartbreak that John and I have experienced for decades, then it must be a good thing.'

Vega acknowledged this with a sad nod. 'No parent should have to go through what you both or the Grants have. But what about the people who killed Hinges? Should they get away with murder?'

'I don't suppose they should, if it were murder,' John said. 'But what if it was self-defence? What if a situation got out of control and they had no choice but to fight back?'

'Then they should have gone to the Gardaí, who would have taken that into account,' Vega replied.

John shrugged. 'Not all situations are clear-cut. Maybe they knew their story would not be believed. And they had a family to protect.'

Vega's eyes locked onto the base of the cherry blossom.

'Oh, Vega,' Anne said, feeling such sympathy for the predicament she was in. 'Do you want to sit down?'

Vega shook her head.

The three of them stood in silence for several minutes, each waiting for another to show their hand.

'What are you going to do?' John asked.

'I don't know,' Vega replied.

'You need to follow your heart. Do what you feel is right,' Anne said. 'It's what I've always done.' Anne shrugged her shoulders apologetically at Vega's tortured face; she was clearly struggling with their revelations.

'I'm sorry . . .' Vega whispered.

'You need to give us some time to prepare the kids before you make any calls,' Anne replied bravely, biting back tears. She needed to be strong – for John and her children – who would need to see she could handle whatever was coming her way.

'I'm going to go home, pour myself a large glass of white and then I'll call my editor,' Vega said.

'And what will you say to him?' John asked.

'I'll update him on today's interview.'

John moved back to Anne and placed a steadying arm round her shoulder. Anne could read him like a book. He was already planning how to confess without implicating her or Michael. Well, he could think again because the only person serving time for this was her.

'I truly am sorry,' Vega continued, her face drawn and tight. She closed her eyes for the briefest moment. 'Because, despite how impressive your fundraising efforts have been here, I will not be including them in my feature.'

'You won't?' Anne whispered.

'No . . .' Vega said, thinking aloud. 'I'm going to write about the current drugs crisis, rather than going back to what happened over thirty years ago. I'll probably just tell my editor that you refused an interview at the last minute. It will be as if I were never here.'

Anne felt her knees buckle, and if John's arms had not been around her she would have collapsed to the ground.

'Why would you do that?' Anne whispered, unable to believe her ears.

Vega approached both of them and reached out to clasp their hands. 'I never had a family growing up, but I used to imagine what they might look like. And when I did they resembled yours. I could never live with myself if I did anything to hurt your family further. Or if I stopped the legacy you are building here.'

'I'd be proud to have a daughter like you,' John said, his voice gruff with emotion.

'Thank you,' Vega replied, then, with one last squeeze of their hands, she turned to walk away. As she moved beneath the heavy arch of a blossom-laden branch, she reached up and plucked a flower. 'I don't know who said this, and I might be misremembering it, but the sentiment feels fitting. Karma has no menu, but you get served what you deserve. I believe that whatever happened to Hinges, he probably received his just desserts.' And then she disappeared down the path.

'I need to sit down,' John said, moving back to the bench.

'Are you okay? You look flushed,' Anne said, reaching up to feel his forehead. 'You don't have any chest pain, do you?'

'It's all right, love. I'm not having a heart attack. Mind you, I think my heart actually stopped there for a minute.'

'Mine too. She reminds me of Margaret, you know,' Anne said approvingly. 'I like her.'

'She's astute. No fooling Vega Pearse. She's a good one.'

'Pity Michael is married. She'd make a wonderful daughter-in-law,' Anne said, gazing longingly towards the path.

'Don't let Michael's wife hear you say that.'

Anne stood up and held her hand out to John. 'Come on, my love. Let's have that fish and chips.'

He took her hand, as he had done for over sixty years, and together they walked along the blossom path home.

About Quick Reads

"Reading is such an important building block for success"

– Jojo Moyes

Quick Reads are short books written by bestselling authors.

Did you enjoy this Quick Read?

Tell us what you thought by filling in our short survey. Scan the QR code to go directly to the survey or visit:
bit.ly/QuickReads2026

Thank you to Penguin Random House, Hachette and all our publishing partners for their ongoing support.

A big thank you to Curtis Brown for supporting the 20th anniversary of Quick Reads.

A special thank you to Jojo Moyes for her generous donation in 2020–2022 which helped to build the future of Quick Reads.

Quick Reads is delivered by The Reading Agency, a UK charity that inspires social and personal change through the proven power of reading.

readingagency.org.uk   @readingagency   #QuickRead

The Reading Agency, Registered number: 3904882 (England & Wales)
Registered charity number: 1085443 (England & Wales)
Registered Office: 24 Bedford Row, London, WC1R 4EH
The Reading Agency is supported using public funding by
Arts Council England.

Find your next Quick Read

For 2026 we have 6 Quick Reads for you to enjoy:

Quick Reads are available to buy in paperback or ebook and to borrow from your local library. For a complete list of titles and more information on the authors and their books visit: **readingagency.org.uk/quickreads**

Continue your reading journey with The Reading Agency:

Reading Ahead

Challenge yourself to complete six reads by taking part in **Reading Ahead** at your local library, college or workplace: **readingahead.org.uk**

Book Club Hub

Join the **Book Club Hub** to find a book club and discover new recommendations: **bookclubhub.co.uk**

World Book Night

Celebrate reading on **World Book Night,** every year on 23 April: **worldbooknight.org.uk**

Summer Reading Challenge

Read with your family as part of the **Summer Reading Challenge**: **summerreadingchallenge.org.uk**

For more information on our work and the power of reading visit: **readingagency.org.uk**

More from Quick Reads

If you enjoyed the 2026 Quick Reads, please explore our 6 titles from 2025:

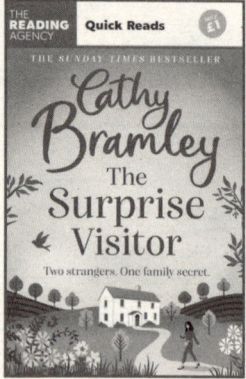
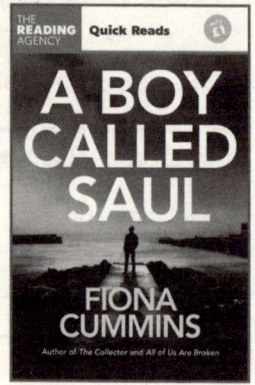

For a complete list of titles and more information on the authors and their books visit: **readingagency.org.uk/quickreads**

Discover more from Carmel Harrington . . .

On a cold afternoon in 1995, two young girls are found abandoned on a train platform.

Thirty years later, journalist Vega is determined to find out what happened to the so-called 'Nowhere Girls'. Where did their mother go? Why did no one come forward to claim them? And where are they now?

But searching for answers will put everything else Vega knows at risk . . .

Copyright © 2026 Carmel Harrington

The right of Carmel Harrington to be identified as the
Author of the Work has been asserted by her in accordance
with the Copyright, Designs and Patents Act 1988.

First published in 2026 by Headline Review
An imprint of Headline Publishing Group Limited

1

Apart from any use permitted under UK copyright law,
this publication may only be reproduced, stored, or transmitted,
in any form, or by any means, with prior permission in writing
of the publishers or, in the case of reprographic production,
in accordance with the terms of licences issued
by the Copyright Licensing Agency.

All characters in this publication are fictitious and any resemblance
to real persons, living or dead, is purely coincidental.

Cataloguing in Publication Data is available from the British Library

Paperback ISBN 978 1 0354 4096 2

Typeset in 12/16pt ITC Stone Serif Std by
Six Red Marbles UK, Thetford, Norfolk

Printed and bound in Great Britain by Clays Ltd, Elcograf S.p.A.

Headline's policy is to use papers that are natural, renewable
and recyclable products and made from wood grown in
well-managed forests and other controlled sources. The logging
and manufacturing processes are expected to conform to the
environmental regulations of the country of origin.

Headline Publishing Group Limited
An Hachette UK Company
Carmelite House
50 Victoria Embankment
London EC4Y 0DZ

The authorised representative in the EEA is Hachette Ireland,
8 Castlecourt Centre, Dublin 15, D15 XTP3, Ireland (email: info@hbgi.ie)

www.headline.co.uk
www.hachette.co.uk